Love,
Katrina
02-24

A Fairy Tale

By

Katrina Bowlin-MacKenzie

Artwork

By

L. Ann Hollingsworth

Published by Katrina Bowlin-MacKenzie

First printing-Aug 2011

Distributed by Createspace.com

ISBN-13:978-1466254558

To contact the author send your emails to;
myst.weaver@yahoo.com

Dedication

This book was written for my daughter,

Charlene almost 30 years ago.

Finally, with the help of L. Ann Hollingsworth

Charlene's book has come alive.

I told you one day it would be done sweetie

I love you

A Fairy Tale

Once upon a time there was a beautiful young girl named Charlene. She went by the name of Charlie.

There was something very special about Charlie.
Charlie could see fairies.

Of course talking to fairies made her different and

because of that, everyone teased Charlie.

Well, Charlie didn't really care that everyone teased her,

because she had her Fairy friends to keep her company.

Would you like to see some of Charlie's Fairy friends?

This is Ariana

This is Gabriana

This is Katriana

Charlie didn't have any friends at school, because

everyone thought she was different.

On the playground at school, Charlie would always sit

by herself under a tree and talk to her Fairy friends.

Do you know why everyone thought Charlie was different.

It was because no one else believed in Fairies.

You can't see something you don't believe in, now can you?

Well, one day Charlie was sitting under her tree, talking to Gabriana, and the other kids were laughing and calling her names.

Katriana was sitting up in the tree and she told Charlie, "Don't you let them bother you Charlie, they just don't understand."

"I know." said Charlie, "sometimes I wish I had real friends, you know, maybe another girl to play with."

"Now don't you worry, Charlie" Said Gabriana, "Somewhere there is another little girl who believes in Fairies.

"There just has to be doesn't there?" Thought Charlie.

Well, life went on for Charlie. The kids teased her and she sat under her tree, every day at recess, talking to...

One day Charlie noticed Traci, the little brown haired girl that lived down the street from her, watching her from behind the school building.

Gabriana asked her "Charlie, do you see Traci watching you?"

"So?" Said Charlie, "She won't talk to me, she never does, no-one does."

Katriana said, "Why don't you call her over, and see if she wants to sit and talk with you?"

"No, you know that no-one likes me or wants to play with me."

"Oh, go on Charlie, give it a try."

Well, Charlie was getting very lonely, so she thought just this once, she would take a chance.

"Hey Traci," called Charlie, "come on over here and sit with me awhile"

Traci was so surprised that she dropped her math book.

"Oh, Charlie." she said "I didn't see you there."

Very slowly, Traci walked over to where Charlie was sitting under her tree. "Is there someone there with you Charlie?" She asked.

"Why do you ask?"

"Well, I thought I heard you talking to someone."

"Do you see anyone?" Charlie asked her. Traci looked around, and didn't see anyone. "Well, if you are alone, I guess I could sit and talk for a while."

Traci and Charlie sat and talked all through recess.

Charlie could see her Fairy friends sitting up in the tree,

but she didn't look at them, or talk to them.

The friendship between Charlie and Traci began to grow, and they spent every recess together, sitting under Charlie's tree and talking.

One day when they were sitting under the tree, Traci

asked Charlie.

"I don't know why the other kids think you are strange, I

like you."

"Really? You like me?"

"Sure I like you, but why do the other kids say that you

talk to Fairies? I don't see you talk to Fairies?"

"Well" Said Charlie. "If I told you that I do talk to

Fairies, would you still be my friend?"

"Sure I would Charlie, you are my best friend."

Do you believe that?

Charlie could see Ariana sitting up in the tree, just fluttering her wings.

and she could see Gabriana sittimg in another part of

the tree.

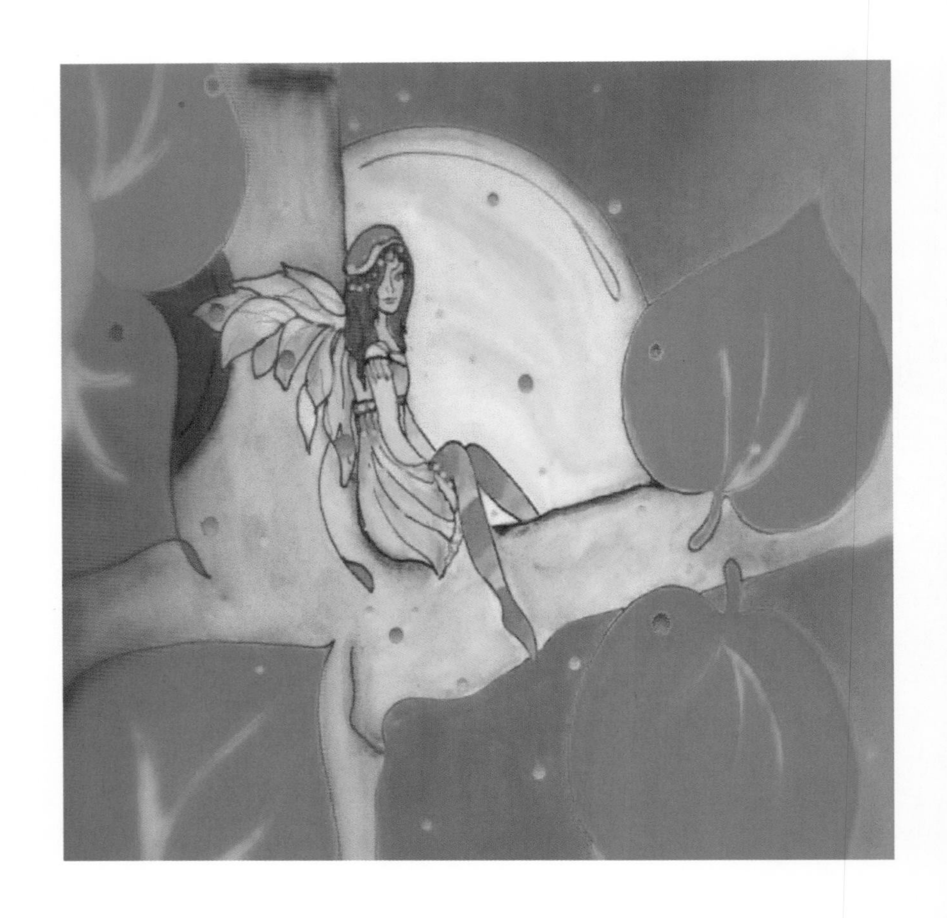

She could even see Katriana sitting in the tree.

They were all smiling and nodding their heads.

"Do you believe in Fairies, Traci?"

"Well, Charlie, I never thought about it, I don't not believe in them. I would love to be able to see Fairies."

"There is one small problem Traci, you can't see Fairies if you don't believe in them."

"Then, help me believe, Charlie, because I want to see Fairies too."

"Traci if you look real hard at that tree, you will be able to see Katriana sitting in it."

It took Traci several days of hard concentration to be able to see Katriana.

But after that, it took only a few minutes to see Ariana

and in no time at all...She could even see Gabriana.

Every day after that, you could always see Charlie and Traci together at recess, sitting under that tree, and talking to someone that no-one else could see.

If you try real hard, maybe you can see.

Just remember, don't let other kids tease you about what you believe in. Be who you are and everything will be just fine....... The end

Katrina is the mother of five wonderful grown children, the grandmother of eleven, (nine grandsons and two granddaughters). Plus she is great grandmother to one very precious little girl.

Her Fae name is Fleur. She is an Intuitive, a Healer, a Psychic Counselor and an author.

Her published works include:

The Beginner's Guide to Psychic Development, published in 2009 by Graveyard Publishing.Ancient Echoes, a paranormal/romance/fantasy, published by Lulu in 2010. My memories of Atlantis are a large part of this book.

She has three children's books completed, but has never been able to find a dedicated artist until recently. The same artist will enable the others to be published soon.

These books were written for my children almost thirty years ago. I promised them that one day they would all come to life, now finally with the help of L. Ann Hollingsworth, that promise is coming true.

All the information on her books is available at her Facebook Author site, Katrina Bowlin-Mackenzie author.

She spends her time writing and designing Gemstone jewelry. She uses Reiki to infuse all her gemstones with healing energy. See her Jewelry page, The Charm Weaver on Facebook. Katrina can be contacted at myst.weaver@yahoo.com or via her Facebook profile.

L. Ann Hollingsworth is an intuitive artist who recently embarked on a journey into the Faerie Realm. She now illustrates books and specializes in the Faes and their magical companions.

L. Ann's background and credentials are in the field of holistic health as an energy practitioner/ Reiki Master, aromatherapist and massage therapist. She also has a BS degree in psychology and counseling experience. She describes this as her 'past life'.

With no background in art, she began to draw in 2006, shortly before a major health crisis. The art became her therapy through the long days of recovery and revealed itself as her 'soul messages' from Spirit. Her mix medium creations are colored pencil, watercolor pencil and acrylics. Filled with bright colors and intuited symbols, L.Ann's joywork carries the essence of the Spirit worlds.

L. Ann states, "Just like Guardian Angels, everyone has a Fae that accompanies them throughout their lifetime – if they will allow. These beings of Light are so excited to join us in creating the new Golden Age of Heaven on Earth. Worlds and dimensions are merging and it is time for us to awaken to the worlds of Magic once again. The Faes are here to help us to do just that.

A Fairy Tale's characters truly exist – Charlie and Traci have really been friends since childhood. Ariana is a beautiful, fair Fae who is caring and encouraging in nature. Gabriana is elegant and wise. Katriana is a young Fae who is full of life and enthusiasm for life."

L.Ann has two sons and one granddaughter, all whom she adores. Her Fae name is "Jewel". She feels as if she is embarking on a new life...and looking forward with great eagerness to where it will lead her....

Please feel free to contact L.Ann Jewel Hollingsworth at lahaha22@hotmail.com or visit her on Facebook. She also created a community page, The Paradise Paradigm, where she shares insights, artwork and new projects.

Printed in Great Britain
by Amazon

20169028R00025